The Disappearance of Drover

The Disappearance
of Drover

John R. Erickson

Illustrations by Gerald L. Holmes

Viking

An Imprint of Penguin Group (USA) Inc.

VIKING
Published by Penguin Group
Penguin Young Readers Group, 345 Hudson Street, New York, New York 10014, U.S.A.
Penguin Group (Canada), 90 Eglinton Avenue East, Suite 700, Toronto, Ontario, Canada M4P 2Y3
(a division of Pearson Penguin Canada Inc.)
Penguin Books Ltd, 80 Strand, London WC2R 0RL, England
Penguin Ireland, 25 St Stephen's Green, Dublin 2, Ireland (a division of Penguin Books Ltd)
Penguin Group (Australia), 250 Camberwell Road, Camberwell, Victoria 3124, Australia
(a division of Pearson Australia Group Pty Ltd)
Penguin Books India Pvt Ltd, 11 Community Centre, Panchsheel Park,
New Delhi – 110 017, India
Penguin Group (NZ), 67 Apollo Drive, Rosedale, Auckland 0632, New Zealand
(a division of Pearson New Zealand Ltd.)
Penguin Books (South Africa) (Pty) Ltd, 24 Sturdee Avenue, Rosebank, Johannesburg
2196, South Africa

Penguin Books Ltd, Registered Offices: 80 Strand, London WC2R 0RL, England

Published simultaneously in the United States of America
by Viking Children's Books and Puffin Books,
divisions of Penguin Young Readers Group, 2011

1   3   5   7   9   10   8   6   4   2

LIBRARY OF CONGRESS CATALOGING-IN-PUBLICATION DATA IS AVAILABLE
ISBN 978-0-14-241845-1 (pbk.) — ISBN 978-0-670-01266-4 (hc.)

Hank the Cowdog® is a registered trademark of John R. Erickson.
Printed in the United States of America

For my grandchildren:
Kale and Alyssa Erickson, and
Cameron and ReAnna Wilson.

CONTENTS

The Disappearance of Drover

This Is the First Chapter

It's me again, Hank the Cowdog. Slim was really steamed when he got to town and figured out that he had two dogs in the back of his pickup, but it wasn't our fault. We had perfectly good reasons for being there, but it might take a while to explain it.

Do we have time to go through all the details that led up to our spending the night in the back of his pickup? Before you answer, let me warn you that it might get pretty scary. And sad. I mean, when Drover vanished without a trace . . .

What do you think? Should we go on with this story or put it in the vault where we keep stories that are too scary or too sad for human consumption? You probably didn't know that we

1

have such a vault, and there's a reason why you don't. Everything that goes into the vault has either been classified Top Secret, Top Sad, or Top Scary, and I'm one of the few dogs on earth that even know it exists.

I'm in on the secret because . . . well, I'm Head of Ranch Security.

It's a huge vault, made of solid steel, and it occupies a whole wall on the twelfth floor of the Security Division's Vast Office Complex. There's only one way in and one way out, and guess whose gunnysack bed is parked right in front of the vault.

Mine. Nobody goes in or comes out without dealing with me. That's how serious we are about the stuff that's locked inside the vault, and that's why I can't tell you about it. As far as you're concerned, it doesn't exist.

Sorry I brought it up. Or, to come at it from another angle, I didn't bring it up. Maybe you thought I did, but I was misquoted. It happens all the time. There is no vault in our Vast Office Complex, and if there were, I couldn't tell you about it. If I did . . . well, we might all be fried for treason.

Tried for freezing.

Tried for treason, there we go. We might all get fried for freezing, and we don't need any of that.

Hmmm. We seem to have gotten off the subject, and I'm not sure where we started. Somehow you coaxed me into talking about the secret vault and . . . wait, here we go.

The story. It's going to get pretty scary and sad, that's the point, so you have to decide whether we should mush on with it or find something else to do. What do you think? Keep going? Are you sure about that?

Well, I guess you're old enough to be making decisions, but if things get out of hand, don't blame me.

Okay, let's set the stage. It was April, as I recall. We'd made it through the worst of the winter and had begun to notice the first signs of spring: buds on the elm trees, flights of cranes honking overhead as they made their way back to the north country, and a number of stopover birds that visit my ranch every fall and spring. They're not invited, but they stop anyway. They occupy my trees, mooch birdseed out of Sally May's feeder, and twitter all day long.

As you might know, I'm not fond of birds, but there's not much I can do about them. If a dog spent all his time barking at birds, he'd have no energy left for the more important jobs, such as barking at the mailman and humbling the cats. Hencely, for a couple of weeks every fall and spring, I have

3

to put up with all their tweeting and twittering.

Drover and I had spent the day at Ranch Headquarters, supervising a project that involved Slim and Loper. They had discovered a spring of water down at the corrals. I mean, all of a sudden and overnight, it had just popped out of the ground and had formed a nice little pool.

In a dry country like ours, you'd think that might be cause for celebration, but it wasn't. Just the opposite, and here's why. Around here, natural springs don't just pop out of the ground, and the cowboys suspected that our bubbling spring had something to do with a leaky water pipe that was buried about three feet underground.

Fellers, you talk about something that will poison the atmosphere on a ranch! An underground water leak will do it, because it involves the use of shovels and manual labor. As you might know, cowboys are allergic to shovels. Bring one out in front of a cowpuncher, and he'll break out in hives.

And mad? They were uncommonly mad. See, the ground in our corrals wasn't what you would call easy digging. Over the years, it had been packed by the hooves of thousands of cattle and horses. If you were going to choose a spot on the ranch where you never wanted to dig a hole, it would be in the middle of the wire lot—exactly where the "spring" had popped out of the ground.

And that's the job I was supervising. You never heard such whining and complaining. It started the moment the first shovel touched the ground and went on most of the afternoon. You want to listen in on some of their conversation? I don't suppose it would hurt anything. Stand by to roll tape.

Transcript of Water Line Episode #205
TOP SECRET

Slim: You know, a guy spends the first half of his life investing in leather and horseflesh and dreaming of the day he can take a real cowboy job, and he spends the second half of his life digging holes in the ground.

Loper: I guess you should have gone to college.

Slim: No, I should have taken a job on a cow outfit where a man can use his horse and rope instead of a frazzling shovel.

Loper: Well, I'd say you're lucky to have a job of any kind. As slow as you dig, we might still be here next Christmas.

Slim: As hard as this ground is, I might not live that long.

Loper: Good. I won't have to send you a Christmas card. It'll save me the cost of a stamp.

Slim: Who laid this stinking waterline anyway?

Loper: My granddaddy.

Slim: Well, I'm going to plant sandburs on his grave for using cheap pipe and covering it up with pavement.

Loper: It was during the Depression, when nobody had two nickels to rub together. They used whatever kind of pipe they could scrounge up. After fifty years, it starts to leak.

Slim: Well, me and your granddaddy have one thing in common: depression. I ain't been so depressed since we had to bail out the septic tank.

Loper: Quit feeling sorry for yourself and dig.

Slim: I am digging, and if I die from heat stroke and overwork, you can push me in this hole and cover me up.

Loper: That would sure cut down on the noise.

Slim: And on my tombstone, you can say, "He always wanted to die ahorseback, but he perished from blisters with a shovel in his hands."

Loper: Slim, just dig the hole.

End of Secret Transcription
Please Destroy at Once

And so forth. They went on like that for hours. In between all the snarling and snapping, they even managed to dig enough of a hole to uncover the rusted waterline that had caused the problem. You probably think they replaced the line with a section of brand-new galvanized pipe. Ha. They fixed it The Cowboy Way, with tar, a strip of inner tube, and a couple of hose clamps.

If they'd asked my opinion, I would have told 'em to fix it right, but they never want to hear any advice from their dogs. Mark my words, next year at this time, they'll find a little spring of water bubbling up in the corrals and we'll have to go through this all over again.

Oh well. I try to run this ranch in a professional manner, but you can only do so much with a couple of knuckleheaded cowboys.

At quitting time, Slim fed the horses and headed for his pickup. Drover and I didn't have any urgent business at Ranch Headquarters, so we decided to hitch a ride and spend the night down at his place.

See, he's a bachelor cowboy and has a very intelligent attitude about dogs. He lets us sleep inside the house. Sometimes he sings to us and shares his supper. Sometimes we have mouse hunts before bedtime, and that's always a lot of fun. The point is that hanging out with Slim is more exciting than occupying a smelly gunnysack bed beneath the gas tanks.

We reached his shack on Wolf Creek around sundown and followed him up to the porch. When he reached for the door handle, Drover and I were poised to dart inside. It's a little game we play, don't you see. The challenge is to see which of us can squirt through the half-opened door and win the I-Got-Here-First Award.

I guess it's kind of silly, but what else does a dog have to do when he lives twenty-five miles out in the country?

So there we were on the porch, poised and quivering with excitement, waiting for Slim to open the door just wide enough so that we could slither inside. But he didn't open the door.

Instead, he looked down at us and gave us a scowl. "Where do you think you're going?"

Well . . . inside the house, of course.

"Uh-uh. It's a nice warm spring evening, and y'all can stay on the porch."

What! Stay on the . . . Drover and I exchanged looks of shock and disappointment.

Slim bent down and looked me in the eye. "You

spent half the day wallering around in that mud hole, pooch. You stink and you ain't going to mess up my nice clean house."

And with that, he went inside, leaving his loyal dogs to sort through the rubble of a shattered dream.

Okay, maybe I'd spent a few minutes in the mud hole . . . a few hours . . . all right, I'd spent most of the afternoon lounging in the water, but when people do that, they call it *a bath*. How's a dog supposed to cleanse his body and wash his hair? When we bathe in the overflow of the septic tank, they complain about that too, so what's a dog supposed to do?

We try so hard to please these people, but sometimes it seems . . . oh well. There's no future in brooding over injustice in the world. It appeared that we would have to spend the night on the porch.

But just as Slim entered the house and closed the screen door behind him, I heard a mysterious ringing sound.

A Trespassing
Badger

Drover heard it, too. "Gosh, what's that?"

"I don't know, but it doesn't sound natural to me."

"Me neither. You reckon we ought to bark?"

"Absolutely, yes. Load up Number Three Barks of Alarm and stand by to fire. Ready? Okay, commence barking!"

Boy, you should have heard us. We spread all four legs, took a firm grip on the porch floor, and rattled the windows with an amazing barrage of . . .

"Hank, knock it off! I'm on the phone."

Huh? Okay, maybe that ringing sound had come from the telephone and, well, we didn't need to waste good barking on that, but a dog can never be sure about those ringing sounds until he checks them out. In the Security Business, we bark first and ask questions later.

I cancelled the alert and moved toward the screen door so that I could hear Slim's side of the conversation. Here's what I heard.

"Lloyd? Well, I'm fine except that we need a rain and I spent most of the day doing plumber work. What? Why yes, I bet I could, and I'd enjoy it, too. Let me check with the boss to be sure. If I don't call you back, I'll be there at ten with a horse. Bye."

He hung up the phone and dialed a number. "Loper? It's me. They're shorthanded at the sale barn and need me to help pen cattle tomorrow. I told Lloyd I'd help him, even though I'd rather stay here and dig sewer lines with you." He laughed, said good-bye, and hung up the phone.

I was sitting in front of the screen door when he came breezing out. The door caught me by surprise and whacked me on the nose. "Out of the way, dogs; I get to play cowboy tomorrow." He stopped and looked down at us. "And y'all can't go. Sorry."

And off he went to feed his horse and hook up the stock trailer.

Well, for his information, I had a long list of jobs to do on the ranch and didn't have time to go chasing off with him to "play cowboy." These people seem to think their dogs just sit around ... hey, I had work to do and a ranch to run, and it sure wasn't going to break my heart if I missed out on his little adventure.

If the dogs don't stay home and keep things running, who will?

So that was the end of it. Slim did his chores, returned to the house, fixed himself a canned mackerel sandwich for supper (we didn't get any of it, not even a bite), and went to bed, leaving the elite troops of the Security Division to sleep on the porch.

It must have been three or four o'clock in the morning when I was awakened by a sound. I lifted my head and focused both ears on a spot of darkness where the sound had ... there it was again, a scratching sound.

Behind me, I heard Drover's voice. "What is that?"

"I don't know, but we're fixing to find out. Form a line. We're moving out."

"It sure is dark."

"Let's go."

We crept off the porch and moved out on silent paws, down the sidewalk, through the yard gate, and into the Great Beyond. We had a sliver of moon, and it gave enough light so that I could see something up ahead. Fifty yards east of the house, I called a halt.

As usual, Drover wasn't paying attention and ran into me. "Oops, sorry."

"Drover, did you see what I saw?"

"I didn't know we had a seesaw."

"We don't have a seesaw. I said, did you see what I saw?"

He blinked his eyes and glanced around. "Well, let me think. I saw your tail, but then it stopped and I ran into it."

"My tail stopped because I stopped. My tail is connected to me, and if you'd pay attention to your business, maybe you'd stop running into me."

"Oh. Sorry. I guess I was thinking about goats."

I looked into the vacuum of his eyes. "Why were you thinking about goats?"

"Oh, I don't know. Elephants are too big and giraffes are too tall, and goats are about the right size to think about."

"Drover, we're on patrol. Stop blabbering and pay attention. Look over there."

He squinted in the direction I was pointing. "I'll be derned. It's a goat."

I stuck my nose in his face. "I don't know what's wrong with you, but that is not a goat. Look again."

"Well . . . it's not a giraffe." He let out a gasp. "Oh my gosh, it's a badger! Last one back to the porch is a rotten egg!"

I caught him just as he was about to run. "Hold your position! If you'll notice, he's only half-grown."

"Yeah, but I know about badgers. They're double-tough."

"Drover, I'll go through this one time, so pay attention. Point One: If you add double-tough and half-grown together, what do you get?"

"Scared?"

"No. You get zero. They cancel each other out. The guy's a shrimp, a zero. Second, there are two of us, which means that we have exactly twice as much firepower as he has."

"Yeah, but . . ."

"Third, he's digging holes in the pasture."

"Fine with me."

"What?"

"I said, what a naughty badger."

"Exactly. What we have here is a shrimpy little badger that's digging holes without a permit, which leads us straight into Point Four: we're fixing to put a stop to this vandalism of ranch property." I laid a paw on his shoulder. "And we need a volunteer."

There was a moment of silence. "You know, I've always dreamed of beating up a badger."

"I like your spirit, son."

"But this old leg's really been giving me fits." He limped around in a circle. "See? Terrible pain."

"Drover, it would look very good on your resume if you beat up a badger. Nobody needs to know that he was a shrimp."

"Yeah, but . . ." He stumbled and fell to the ground. "Drat the luck, there went the leg! Maybe you'd better take this one."

"All right, you little faker. I'll take the lead position, and we'll hold you in reserve."

"Let's don't hurt him. He's just a little guy."

"We'll give him whatever it takes to send him on his way. Let's move out."

We crept forward. Up ahead, we could see the badger digging. They're famous diggers, you know. They've got long claws and powerful front legs. Give a badger a couple of hours and he'll dig up half an acre of pasture.

What are they digging for? Who knows?

Probably bugs. I don't care what kind of excuse they come up with. If they don't have a permit to dig, they need to move along.

About ten yards away from the target, I stopped and took another look. "Abel Baker, this is Baker Charlie. The package appears to be, uh, bigger than we thought."

"Yeah, but he's not as big as a goat. And I bet he'll run. They always run back to their holes."

I gave that some thought. "Good point. Okay, I'll give him a stern barking. In the event that he wants to fight, we'll, uh, melt back to the porch. What do you think?"

"That'll work."

"All right, here I go. If I encounter any problems, I'll call for backup. Stay alert."

"Got it."

The badger was so busy digging and sniffing and destroying ranch property, he never saw me coming. Good. I crept up behind him, filled my lungs with a fresh supply of air, squared my enormous shoulders, and gave him a blast of barking.

Heh heh. That woke him up. He whirled around, saw me towering over him (badgers are built low to the ground, don't you know), and off he went, running as fast as his stubby legs would

carry him—not very fast. I could have rolled him easy, but . . . well, we wanted to avoid a confrontation if at all possible. I mean, he wasn't the biggest badger I'd ever seen, but he was still a badger.

I reached for the radio. "Hank to Drover, over. The package is moving. Let's give pursuit and see where he goes."

"Got it."

This promised to be a routine assignment with no major bloodshed. I hit an easy trot and followed the culprit. I would give him a scare and a warning ticket and that would be the end of it.

He hadn't gone more than, oh, thirty yards when he came to his hole and dived inside. I was standing over the hole when Drover came up, huffing and puffing. "Did he go in the hole?"

"That's correct. I guess he didn't want a piece of me." I glanced at Drover and saw that he was wearing an odd smile. "What are you grinning about?"

"Oh, I was just thinking . . . maybe we could dig him out."

"Dig him out? Why would we want to do that?"

He let out a giggle. "Hee hee. 'Cause there's two of us and only one of him. 'Cause he's a little shrimp. 'Cause it might be fun."

I gave that some thought. "You know, you're right, it might be fun. I mean, if he's in the hole and we're outside, what harm can come of it? You want to dig or should I?"

I was shocked when he said, "Oh, I'll do it. I'm feeling kind of wild." He puffed himself up and took a step toward the hole . . . and let out a groan. "Uh-oh, there's that leg again. Maybe I'd better give it some rest."

"Drover, one of these days I'm going to get suspicious about your leg. Get out of the way." I pushed him aside and stepped up to the hole.

"No, this time it's real pain, and it's really painful."

"Please hush, I'm trying to concentrate."

I started digging, and we're talking about dirt flying in all directions. Hey, this was fun! After moving several cubic yards of dirt, I stuck my nose into the hole and delivered a blast of barking. "This is Ranch Security, so listen up! The next time you want to tear up ranch property . . ."

Huh?

CHAPTER THREE

The Pit
of Death

We need to say a few words about badgers. When a dog runs a half-grown badger down a hole, he has every reason to suppose that the hard part is over. What remains is good clean entertainment for the dogs. We bark for a while, then go back to the house, right?

That's what I had in mind, but what I hadn't counted on—and what no dog would have considered—was that we had crossed paths with a half-grown badger who was also a little hoodlum with no respect for authority.

You know what he did? He grabbed my ears with both paws and *started pulling me down into his hole!* Oh, and he started hissing, too. In case you've never shared a hole with an angry badger,

let me point out that they can hiss like . . . I don't know what, but it sounded like there were twenty-three hissing cobras inside that hole.

Fellers, you talk about something that will throw a dog into Panic Overload. That did it. I hit Full Reverse on all engines and started throwing up dirt with all four legs. "Drover, send troops, we've been ambushed! Help!"

Did the troops arrive just in time to save my skin? Of course not. Drover vanished like a puff of smoke, and the badger kept pulling me deeper into the Pit of Death. Huge badger, biggest one I'd ever encountered.

Oh, and you know what else he did? He bit me on the lip and wouldn't let go! No kidding, he actually put a fang-lock on my lip and hung on, and how's a dog supposed to defend himself when he's got a badger on his lip? At that point I knew that the time had come to, uh, settle this thing out of court, so to speak.

"Hey listen, pal, I think we got the wrong address, no kidding. See, we were looking for a gopher and, well, ha ha, it's pretty clear that you're not . . . hey, buddy, will you let go of my lip?"

Before you mess around with a badger, you should understand that they don't negotiate. They don't talk or listen or compromise, and they have no sense of humor. Zero. When they get stirred up enough to pull you down into a hole, they're not kidding.

It was a good thing he was only half-grown, because if he'd been full-grown, I would have been dragged down into The Place Where No Dog Wants to Go and this story wouldn't have a happy ending.

I don't know what saved me (it wasn't Drover), but all at once the little thug let me go. Since I had all four legs in Full Reverse, I went flying out of the hole and did two backward rolls. I staggered to my feet, blinked my eyes, and stood there, quivering all over. Somehow I had managed to survive one of the most terrifying ordeals of my whole career and . . . and I should have just walked away and left it there. However . . .

This is really hard to explain. See, when a dog survives a terrible ordeal, it gives him a rush of adrinkalot . . . androidin . . . it gives him a rush of some kind of juice that makes him feel like King Kong.

Adrenalin, there we go. His glandular so-forths pump large quantities of the harmonicas . . . hormones, let us say . . . into his bloodstream and . . . well, sometimes it makes him do things that are really dumb.

I hate to put it that way, but how else do you explain . . . see, instead of walking away and calling it good, I just couldn't resist . . . I marched back to the hole, stuck my head inside, and yelled, "Okay, you little creep, you beat me with that lip-lock, but if you ever come out of that hole again . . ."

HERE HE CAME! And we're talking about red-hot lava rushing up from the center of the earth. I won't try to sugarcoat this next part. I did what a brave ranch dog never wants to do. I pushed the throttle up to Turbo Seven and ran for my life.

It was total defeat and humiliation. The Security Division left the field of battle in panic and disarray.

Whew! Boy, what a dragon. I headed straight for the house. If the badger had followed me, I might have been forced to dive through a window and take refuge under Slim's bed, but lucky for me, he quit the chase and I settled for leaping into the back of the pickup, which was parked beside the house.

I scrambled over the tailgate and squeezed myself into a corner behind the cab. There, in the eerie silence, I caught my breath and tried to absorb the powerful lesson that had come from my ordeal. You want to hear it?

Even the Head of Ranch Security needs to learn when to keep his big mouth shut.

Yes, it was a powerful lesson and I will never remember it.

Never forget it, shall we say.

After absorbing that powerful lesson, I found myself . . . well, worrying about Drover. I know I shouldn't have wasted my time. The little goof had left me hung out to dry, but still . . . great generals always worry about their men. Think of the ones we remember from history: Napoleon, Seizure of Rome, Salamander the Great, Charlie Mange. . . . All those guys worried about the common soldiers who marched into battle and served with distinction.

Come to think of it, Drover hadn't done either one of those things, but I worried about him anyway. What if he'd been mugged by the badger . . . or eaten alive? I waited and listened (nothing, not a sound), and with each passing second, my head grew heartier . . . my heart grew heavier, let us say, until I could no longer endure the strain.

I rose to a standing position and peered over the side of the pickup bed. "Drover? Pssst. Are you out there?"

I cocked my ear and waited, and began picking up an odd thumping sound in the night. What was that? I listened closer and there it was again. It sounded a bit like . . . huh? Okay, relax. Ha ha. It was the sound of my own . . . ha ha. You know, in times of stress, a guy can hear his own heart beating and . . . skip it.

The point is that I heard almost nothing at all, and certainly no trace of the guy whose fate had become a matter of great concern. "Drover? Are you there?"

And that's when I heard a tiny voice in the distance. "Yes! I'm here!"

"Oh, thank goodness! I've been worried about you."

"Thanks. Me, too."

"Remember that little badger?"

"Oh yeah."

"Well, he turned out to be a lot tougher than we thought."

"I'll be derned. Did you beat him up?"

There was a moment of silence. "We'll talk about it later. Are you all right?"

"Well, this old leg's still giving me fits, but I guess I'm okay."

"Good. Listen, I've taken refuge in the back of Slim's pickup. With that badger on the loose, I think we should camp here for the night. Can you find it in the dark?"

"Already did."

"What? Come back on that."

"I've been here for fifteen minutes."

"Yes, but where is here? Be specific, son, we need details."

"Three feet to your left."

"What! You have only three feet left? I thought you said . . ."

"Turn to the left."

I turned to the left. "Roger that. Now what?"

"Look straight ahead."

I narrowed my eyes and peered into the darkness directly in front of me and saw. . . . "Drover? Is that you?"

"Yeah. Hi."

I marched over to him and snarled in his face. "Listen, you little pipsqueak, that badger pulled me into his hole and almost chewed my lip off."

"You mean . . ."

"Yes! I called for backup, and what did you do?"

"Well, I backed up . . . all the way here."

"Exactly, and for that, you will receive five Chicken Marks."

"Drat."

"Make it six, one for naughty language. And tomorrow, you will stand with your nose in the corner."

He cried and moaned and begged me not to give him the Chicken Marks, but my heart had turned to stone. By George, if we don't stand firm and impose discipline, who will teach the Drovers of this world how to behave?

Well, we had both escaped with our lives. A few minutes before daylight, we had accounted for all our troops and hunkered down for a few hours of well-deserved sleep.

And in case you were worried about my lip, yes, it hurt.

Pretty scary, huh? I tried to warn you. It had been a long and brutal campaign for those of us in the Security Division. We'd taken some hits and suffered some indignities, but against incredible odds, we'd survived to fight another day.

Little did we know or suspect that . . . well, you'll see.

CHAPTER FOUR

The Rubber Baby-
Buggy Bumpers

Ordinarily, I'm the first one out of bed, and we're talking about early, four–five o'clock in the morning, the darkness before dawn. I take pride in being the first one up and kind of enjoy telling everyone that by seven o'clock, I've already put in half a day's work.

But the day of which we're whiching began a little different. In the first place, I didn't leap out of bed at my usual time. I didn't bark up the sun or chase the wild turkeys. I slept late, and I'm not proud to admit it. I mean, Drover is easily corrupted and I try to set a good example, but on this particular morning, I kind of went to seed.

There were reasons for it, of course. Don't forget that I had been up half the night doing battle with

30

a ferocious badger. Show me a dog that fights full-grown badgers and I'll show you a dog that doesn't jump out of bed at the crack of dawn. Even a body that's made of iron and steel will show the effects of badger-fighting, and mine did.

So I gave my aching body a little vacation from the endless routine of running the ranch and stayed in bed. I was awakened by an odd sensation. I felt that I was . . . well, moving.

I raised my head, blinked my eyes, and glanced around. What I saw was astounding. My bedroom had been transformed into a kind of metal container, but without a roof. I could see the sky overhead and feel wind rushing past my ears. And directly to my left, I saw . . . what was that thing? It appeared to be a pile of hair.

Well, you know me. When I wake up and see an unauthorized pile of hair, I don't just sit there looking simple. I grabbed the microphone of my mind and put in an urgent call to Data Control.

"Spaghetti Central, this is Whickerbill. Corned beef is tadpoling the rubber baby-buggy bumpers!"

I waited for a reply, but the line seemed to have gone dead. That's the problem with this modern technology. Just when you really need it, it goes on the blink. I would have to work this out on my own.

I moved closer to the pile of hair and gave it a

sniffing with Nosetory Scanners. It had a familiar smell, but I couldn't come up with any kind of solid identity. At that point, it appeared to be . . . well, just a random pile of hair.

But then, before my very eyes, the pile of hair transformed into something with two eyes, two ears, and a nose. It appeared to be some kind of life-form. It blinked its eyes, grinned, and spoke. "Oh, hi. Is it morning already?"

"Who are you, and what have you done with the rubber baby-buggy bumpers?"

"Well, I'm Drover, and I don't know anything about rubby bigger-baby bippers."

"You're Drover? Then what . . ." I glanced around. "Drover, something has happened to our bedroom. Everything's changed, and I have the strangest feeling that . . . well, that we're moving."

He stood up and looked around. "Yeah, 'cause we are."

"But how can that be?"

"Well, we spent the night in the back of Slim's pickup, and I think we're going to town."

"Really?" I went to the side of the pickup bed and saw a highway rushing past. "Drover, it's coming back to me now. I got mugged by a badger, and we spent the night in the pickup, remember? And now the pickup is moving. I think we're heading for town."

"Yeah, and Slim's going to be surprised when he finds us back here."

I began pacing, as I often do when I'm dealing with large concepts. "Okay, there's just one thing that doesn't add up. I can accept that we're in a moving pickup. I can accept that we're going to town, but I don't understand the connection with rubber baby-buggy bumpers."

Drover shrugged. "Yeah, that's a toughie."

You know, we never did figure it out and it remains a mystery to this very day. Neither of us ever figured out who stole the rubby bubby-baby bumpers, or why. But once I had cleared the sleep and cobwebs out of my head, one fact remained clear and true.

WE WERE GOING TO TOWN! And if you're a ranch dog, going to town is a big deal.

See, we lived twenty-five miles from Twitchell and spent most of our time working hard to protect our ranch. Well, I did. Drover spent most of his time goofing off and chasing butterflies, while I worked eighteen hours every day to protect my ranch from coyotes, cannibals, raccoons, skunks, porcupines, and badgers.

And speaking of badgers, my nose and ears still throbbed from the . . . he'd caught me by surprise, is how he did it, and landed a few lucky punches; but if I ever caught him on my place again, he would face an older, wiser, meaner Hank the Cowdog, and he would be in deep trouble.

Anyway, we dogs didn't have many opportunities to visit the big city of Twitchell, and, to be honest, we were seldom invited. That always seemed odd to me. I mean, you'd think our people would want to show us off to the general public and would be proud to drive down Main Street with a couple of high-dollar ranch dogs in the back of the pickup.

That's what you'd think, but they rarely invited us to go with them on their trips to town. Slim hadn't invited us this time either, but that was just his tough luck. I had every intention of making the most of it.

Thirty minutes after leaving the ranch, we drove past the Twitchell City Limits sign, POP. 1,377, and made our way down the main thoroughfare of this huge city. It had been a while since I'd been to town, but right away I saw familiar sights that brought back pleasant memories: Waterhole 83, the Dixie Dog Drive-in, and Jim's Tire Shop. Off in the distance, I could see the yard where I had saved my sister Maggie from the notorious Car Barkaholic Dog. (*Rambo. Remember him?*)

Over in the other direction, I caught sight of a place that brought back memories that weren't so pleasant: the Twitchell Dog Pound, otherwise known as Devil's Island for Dogs. Yes, I had spent some time in that . . . you know, we probably shouldn't be talking about this (the little children), so for the record, let's just say that I'd heard about the place and about the guy who ran it (Jimmy Joe Dogcatcher), and it was no place where a respectable dog wanted to spend any time.

There. Let the record state that I knew almost nothing about Devil's Island for Dogs.

As we cruised down Main Street, Drover and I sat up and gawked at all the wonderful sights. By the time we had reached the stoplight in the middle of town, I had decided to give Drover a history lesson. I mean, the little mutt had lived a sheltered life and needed to expand his tiny mind.

"Drover, do you realize that Twitchell was one of the first towns ever built in Texas?"

He had been staring off into space. His gaze drifted down and landed on me. "Oh, hi. Did you say something?"

"I did, yes. We're going to begin our unit on Texas history."

"Well, I'm kind of busy right now."

"You're not busy. You're just sitting there like a stump, and you might as well learn something."

"Oh, rats."

"What?"

"I said, Oh, yes."

"That's the spirit. In today's lesson, we learn that Twitchell was one of the first towns ever built in Texas."

"I'll be derned. How'd you know that?"

"I know it because I observe. I pay attention. While you were in your dreamy state, we passed five buildings that should have given you a clue. Did you notice even one of them?"

He glanced around. "Well, I saw the Dixie Dog."

"That wasn't one of them. Now pay attention. In the last five minutes, we have passed the First National Bank, the First State Bank, the First Methodist church, the First Baptist church, and the First Christian church."

"You mean . . ."

"Exactly. Those were the first churches and banks ever built in Texas. Following the path of simple logic, we must conclude that Twitchell is the oldest town."

He was impressed. "I'll be derned. History's all around us."

"Yes indeed. Twitchell is not only older than

Austin and San Antonio, it might even be older than dirt."

"Yeah, I just saw a street that wasn't paved."

"Exactly my point. It was a dirt street, and it's been here since the very day dirt was invented."

His face bloomed in a smile. "You know, I never cared much for history, but it's pretty interesting."

I gave him a pat on the shoulder. "Stick with me, son, and you'll learn a lot. With me, the education never stops."

You know, a lot of dogs wouldn't have taken the time to school Drover. They'd have seen him as a hopeless case. To be honest, there had been times when I'd considered him a hopeless case, but those of us who live on the mountaintop have a responsibility to help our fellow dogs; and any time I can drag Drover up the Hill of Knowledge, I'm glad to do it.

Okay, I'm not exactly *glad* to do it, but I do it.

That was a pretty awesome history lesson, wasn't it? You bet. And now you know that Twitchell was the very first town in Texas. What you don't know is that the citizens of Twitchell were having a big parade that day, and I probably shouldn't tell you who or whom they were honoring.

Or maybe I will. Me. No kidding.

CHAPTER FIVE

My
Parade

It came as a complete surprise. I mean, nobody had said a word to me about the parade, and I was . . . well, you can imagine. Proud but also very surprised, and humbled. Here's what we saw as we drove down the main street of the oldest town in Texas.

We were sitting at the stoplight, the one that sits in the middle of town, and Drover's ears shot up. "Hey, I hear drums."

I hoisted up my left ear and twisted it around. "Hmm, it does sound like drums. Why would we be hearing drums at this time of day?"

"I don't know. What time is it?"

"It's too early for drums. Nobody beats on drums in the morning."

Drover listened some more. "Yeah, but somebody is. And you know what else? I think it's a marching band."

"Impossible." I hopped my front legs on the side of the pickup bed and looked up ahead. "Holy smokes, it *is* a marching band, and look at all the people lining the street. Drover, this is a parade!"

"I'll be derned. How fun. I wonder what they're celebrating."

We had left the stoplight by this time and were creeping down the street behind the marching band. On both sides of the street, throngs of people waved and cheered. Above the roar of the crowd, I heard a child exclaim, "Oh, look at the dog!"

That's when I figured it out. "Drover, is it possible that they're giving this parade for us?"

"Oh, I don't think so."

"Then why are they here at this time of day? Why did they let the children out of school? Why are they cheering and looking at us?"

"Well . . ."

I turned to the crowd on the east side of the street and waved. "Thank you so much! I'm speechless." I whirled back to Drover. "Don't you get it? They heard about my Badger Campaign. Someone must have told them I was coming to town."

"Yeah, but nobody knew about it."

I faced the crowd again and blew them a kiss. "Thank you, thank you! You know, Drover, words fail me at times like this. All my life I've tried to be a good example for the little children, and now . . . just look at them! They've turned out in droves . . . and listen to their shouts of joy and admiration!"

"Yeah, but I don't think it's for us."

"It's for ME. Don't forget who's Head of Ranch Security." I turned back to the cheering throngs and waved. "Thank you! You're all wonderful!" Back to Drover. "Slim must have arranged it, and the rascal never said a word about it."

Drover pointed to a banner that had been hung across the street. "Yeah, but look at that."

I narrowed my eyes and studied the lettering on the banner. It said, *Welcome Home AA State Basketball Champs.* "Okay, so there's a banner. What's your point?"

"Well, we don't play basketball."

"Drover, that banner has probably been there for years. Don't you remember seeing it the last time we were in town?"

"Not really."

"Well, I do. This parade has nothing to do with . . ." Just then, I caught sight of a very

41

attractive lady dog sitting on the curb. I rushed to the side of the pickup and beamed her a wolfish smile. "Good morning, my lovely sugarplum! This is very impressive, isn't it? I'm so glad you could come and share my day of triumph."

I blew her a kiss, and she . . . well, she laughed and I wasn't sure what that meant, but when the women are laughing, it's no bad deal.

I turned back to Drover and noticed that he had shrunk down behind the side of the pickup bed, almost as though he was . . . well, hiding. "Hey, you're missing the show. I know it's all for me, but I don't mind sharing a piece of it with you."

"Well, this old leg started acting up, and I needed to lie down."

"Drover, this is so overwhelming, it almost brings tears to my . . ." At that very moment, I caught sight of two scruffy dogs on the edge of the crowd. They were smirking and pointing at me. I knew them: Buster and Muggs.

Remember Buster and Muggs? They were stray dogs, tough guys who made their living tipping over garbage barrels, and I'd had a few encounters with them—enough to know that I didn't like them.

And there they were, down in the dust of the street while I passed by in my open limousine. A sudden impulse seized me and I made an ugly face at them, crossed my eyes, and stuck out my tongue. And I yelled, "What do you think, guys? Anybody ever throw a parade for you? Ha ha."

Drover had been watching, and he started fretting. "Hank, I don't think you ought to be saying things like that. You might make 'em mad."

"Hey, this is my parade, and I can do whatever I want." I turned back to the mutts and yelled, "Come around after the show and maybe I'll give you an autograph!"

Hee hee. That really got Muggsie wired up. He was Buster's stooge, don't you know, and he thought he was hot stuff. He started bouncing up and down, and talking trash.

Buster gave me a sour look and yelled, "Cowdog, you're such a loser! You ain't got sense enough to pour sand out of a boot!"

"Oh yeah? Tell that to the citizens of this town, Buster. Tell it to all the mothers who brought their little children to see a dog whose life has made a difference. Oh, and by the way, Buster, when are they going to have your parade, huh?"

Boy, I got 'em told, and all they could do was sit there and take it. Hee hee. I loved it. One of the great things about being in a parade is that you don't have to be humble about it. Most of the time, humble is the best course, but once in a while a guy can't resist mouthing off.

Well, this outpouring of support from the community was almost overwhelming, but all good things must end. At the north end of town, the band halted, broke ranks, and melted away, the kids carrying their horns and drums. Many of them saw me standing tall in the back of the pickup and waved a last farewell. I'm sure it was a day they would always remember and cherish.

Slim sped up, turned left, and headed for the livestock auction on the north edge of town. I heaved a sigh and turned to my companion. "Isn't it touching that Slim planned all this?"

"Yeah, especially since he doesn't even know we're back here."

The smile I had been wearing began to fade. "Hmm. That's an interesting point. To be honest, I hadn't thought of that. Do you suppose . . ."

"They had a parade for the basketball team. We just got stuck in the traffic."

"What are you saying, Drover? Are you trying to tell me . . ."

"It wasn't for you."

Huh? My mind swirled. "But everyone was laughing. They seemed so happy. Surely they weren't . . ." I began pacing, as I often do when

Life has dealt me a blow. "Drover, I've been the victim of a cruel hoax. That parade was for the basketball team."

"That's what I said."

"And maybe I shouldn't have run my mouth off to Buster and Muggs."

"Yeah, you get carried away."

"I mean, a guy shouldn't go out of his way to make enemies."

"I tried to tell you."

I whirled around and gave him a ferocious glare. "Why didn't you tell me? You just sat there and let me make a fool of myself!"

"You'd better hide before Slim sees us."

"Don't tell me what to do!" I took a deep breath and tried to calm myself. "Maybe we'd better hide. If Slim finds us back here, he'll blow a gasket."

Anyway, we'd got caught in a traffic jam, and it took us a while to make our way down Main Street. Traffic jams aren't too common in Twitchell, but this one had something to do with . . . I don't know, the local basketball team had done something and I guess the town thought it was a big deal. If you ask me . . . never mind.

At last we made it to the livestock auction, and Slim pulled into the parking lot. Even though the sale didn't start for another half-hour, the parking lot was filling up with pickups of all colors and sizes, and most of them were hooked up to stock trailers.

Do you know why? Because most of the people who attend a livestock auction are either buying or selling cattle. If they're selling, they haul their stock into town in a trailer. If they're buying, they'll need a trailer to haul their cattle back to the ranch.

It's kind of impressive that a dog would know so much about the business, isn't it? A lot of mutts (Drover, for example) don't pay any attention to the details of livestock marketing, but the Head of Ranch Security needs to have a pretty firm grisp of the Big Picture.

So there we were. Slim parked in the shade of a scraggly Chinese elm tree and shut off the motor. At that point, I knew that we had reached a crucial point in this adventure. If he saw us in the back of the pickup, he would throw a fit and we would have to listen to him fume and bellow, so I gave Drover the signal to move into the Stealth Configuration.

Have we discussed SC? Maybe not. It's a special technique we use in delicate situations when our presence might not, uh, cause the hearts of our people to sing with joy, let us say. In SC, we lie flat and put all systems on lockdown. We don't move a hair or make a sound. We become Invisible Dogs and even radar can't find us.

We initiated SC and waited in the brittle silence. Slim opened his door and got out. We heard the crunch of his boots on the gravel. He went to the back of the stock trailer and unloaded his horse. So far, so good.

At that point, we heard the door of the auction barn open and close. Someone had come outside, and he spoke to Slim. "Morning. You ready to pen some cattle?"

"You bet. Sorry I'm late, but I got caught on the tail end of a parade."

"Yeah, our boys won state. Well, come on and I'll get you set up."

The footsteps moved away from us. Our Stealth Program had worked to perfection, but then . . . I couldn't believe this! You won't believe it either. Drover picked this time, of all times, to hiccup!

CHAPTER SIX

Drover
Disappears

"H ICK!"
    The footsteps stopped and Slim said,
"What was that?"

"I didn't hear anything."

There was a moment of tense silence, then
they began walking away from us again. Whew! It
appeared that we had dodged a bullet.

"HICK!"

I couldn't believe it! I gave the runt a scorching
glare that said, "What's wrong with you!" And he
gave me a pitiful look that said, "I couldn't help it."

Oh brother! The footsteps stopped and the
other man said, "I heard it that time. It came from
your pickup."

"Huh. You don't reckon . . ."

The footsteps were coming in our direction. Well, Drover had blown our cover and we were about to be exposed. I switched off Stealth and went into a routine called "We Don't Know How We Got Here, Honest." (We shorten it to "WDKHWGHH," which is pronounced "Wuh-Duh-Kuh-Huh-Wuh-Guh-Huh-Huh") In Wuh-Duh-Kuh-Huh-Wuh-Guh-Huh-Huh, we go to Sad Eyes and Mournful Thumps of the tail, and hope for the best. Sometimes it works and sometimes it doesn't.

Seconds later, Slim's face appeared over the side of the pickup bed. When he saw us, his eyebrows rose, then fell into an avalanche of wrinkles. "I ain't believing this." He rolled his eyes up to the sky, rocked up and down on his toes, and muttered something I couldn't hear. I held my breath and waited for the fire and brimstone. I knew it was coming.

After a moment of deadly silence, Slim's gaze sliced through the air and landed on. . . . Why was he glaring at ME? The guy who'd hiccupped was sitting right beside me. Could we glare at him?

"All right, geniuses, you're here and there's nothing I can do about it. I've got to pen cattle behind the auction barn, and I won't be done till four o'clock. Stay in the pickup and don't bark. Understand?"

I gave my tail three slow taps. Yes sir.

Slim's eyes narrowed and he looked closer at . . . well, at my face, it seemed. "What happened to your nose? Looks like you stuck it in a lawn mower."

Well, there was this badger, see, and . . .

"Try to act your age, not your IQ. Bozo."

And that was it. He left, walked away and led his horse to the pens behind the sale barn.

You see how they treat their dogs? Hey, there was a very good reason why my nose had taken a beating. I'd been protecting his ranch from . . . oh well.

I whirled around to Drover. "Well, thanks a lot, you little goofball. We were home free, had it made, but then you just had to hiccup."

"It slipped out, sorry."

"And, as if that weren't enough, you did it a second time! What's wrong with you?"

His head sank. "I don't know. Sometimes I just lose control of myself."

I rose to my feet and began pacing back and forth in front of him. "That's exactly right. You have no control over your life, and that's why your life is out of control."

"It was just a hiccup."

"Drover, today it was a hiccup. Tomorrow it

might be something far worse. Until you take control of your . . . hick . . . impulses, you'll never amount to a hill of bones."

"You mean beans?"

"Mean beans? What are you talking about?"

"You said I'll never amount to a hill of bones, but I think you meant a hill of beans."

"That's what I said: you'll never amount to a hick of bricks."

He stared at me and grinned. "Did you hiccup?"

"No, I did not. Don't try to change the subject, and wipe that silly smick off your licks."

"You did hiccup."

I looked into the vacuum of his eyes. "Drover, I'm trying to hick you . . . help you. The sad truth is that you'll never go anywhere in the Security Division until you learn to contrick your basic impulses. Hick."

"I think you've got the hiccups."

"I do not have the hiccups! Are you trying to make a mockery of my life? Because, if you are . . . hick . . . let me remind you that . . . hick . . ." I stuck my nose in his face and screamed, "You see what you've done? You ruined my parade and now you're trying to . . . hick. Never mind, just skip it."

I stormed away from the little lunatic, went all the way to the back of the pickup bed, as far away from him as I could get. There, I sat down and tried to reorganize the scattered papers of my mind.

You know, there are times when I think that Drover has some kind of dark, mysterious power that can turn a normal situation into a disaster. I'd seen it before and it had alarmed me, but this latest outburst really gave me a jolt. Somehow, through some kind of hickery . . . excuse me . . . through some kind of trickery, he had managed to turn my lecture into rubble.

I mean, when your lecture on hiccups turns into a full-blown case of hiccups . . . fellers, that's creepy. I had no idea how he'd pulled it off, but one thing became very clear to me. The Security Division had no place for a mutt who went around sowing the seeds of chaos.

As of that very moment, Drover was off the payroll, fired. Not only was he off the force, but I would never speak to him ahick . . . speak to him again.

It was a tough decision and it brought me no pleasure, but it had to be done. If we allow the forces of chaos to hick . . .

This is ridiculous.

Where were we? Oh yes, Drover had been court-martialed and dismissed from the force.

I remained on my end of the pickup bed and he stayed on his end, and I didn't even look at him. My hiccups went away and my life returned to normal. I was ready to settle down for a nice long nap . . . when I heard Drover's voice.

"I wonder how old Mom's doing. I haven't seen her in ages." I ignored him but he kept yapping. "The livestock auction reminds me of her. She made me come here and apply for a dog-job. Boy, that was a flop. I knew it would be and tried to tell her, but she'd got it in her head that I needed a job."

I cracked my eyes and lifted my head. "Are you talking to someone in particular or just blabbering?"

His gaze drifted down from the clouds. "Oh, hi. Did you just get here?"

"No. I've been here since last night. I spent the night in this pickup. So did you."

"Oh yeah. Boy, time sure flies."

"I was trying to take a nap, but you started yapping."

"I did?"

"Something about your mother."

A dreamy look came into his eyes. "Yeah, good old Mom. I wish I could go by and see her."

"Yes, but you can't. Slim gave us strict orders

to stay in the pickup. He'll be penning cattle for hours."

"She always hoped I'd become a good little doggie."

I heaved a weary sigh, pushed myself up to a standing position, and walked over to him. "Hello? Is anybody home?"

"Oh yeah, she never leaves her yard."

"Drover, snap out of it. You can't visit your mother, and I can't sleep while you're blabbering. Lie down and be quiet. One more outburst and I'll have to write you up."

"Oh, sorry."

"Thank you." I returned to my spot and flopped down.

"You're welcome."

"Drover, please hush."

At last he zipped his mouth, and I was able to grab a few winks of wonderful sleep. Don't forget that I'd been up half the night fighting badgers, so my body was . . . We've already discussed that.

For a solid hour, I slept like a rock, but then I was awakened by a crazy dream. I dreamed that Drover and I were in town, in the back of Slim's pickup, and he hopped out and went to visit his mother.

Ha ha. It's funny how your mind plays tricks,

isn't it? The odds of Drover doing something like that were somewhere between zero and nothing. I mean, the guy was a complete scaredy-cat, and he knew that town could be a dangerous place: traffic, strangers, and stray dogs. Oh, and don't forget the dogcatcher who snatched up unwary mutts and hauled them off to prison.

Drover wasn't the sharpest tool in the shop, but he had a natural allergy to anything that carried the slightest whiff of danger, so I woke up laughing at my own silly dream. "Hey Drover, you'll never guess what I just dreamed. Ha ha. It's the craziest thing you ever heard. I dreamed . . ."

I blinked my eyes and glanced around. Unless my eyes were deceiving me, the pickup bed was empty . . . well, except for me. "Drover?" Nothing, not a sound. "Drover, return to base immediately, and that is a direct order! If you don't report back in one minute, you will be AWOL." Still not a sound. "Drover, this isn't funny. I'm going to count to three, and you'd better be front and center when I get done."

I yelled out the count and by the time I got to "three," the awful truth had begun to soak in. The little mutt had done the unthinkable, and all at once my dream didn't seem nearly as crazy as it should have been. Little Drover was now running loose in a huge city, and it was just a matter of time until . . .

Well, all I could say was "Good-bye, Drover, and good luck." There wasn't a thing I could do about it. He had disobeyed orders and made one of the dumbest decisions on record, and now he would have to live with the results.

I was pretty sure it would be bad. I just hoped it wouldn't be fatal.

And so it was that I began preparing myself for Life Without Drover. It would be peaceful and free of many annoyances. I wouldn't have to listen to him wheeze and yip in his sleep, send him to his room, or make him stand with his nose in the corner.

I wouldn't have to keep track of all his Chicken Marks or dig him out of his Secret Sanctuary in the machine shed.

Scrap Time would be a much more pleasant occasion, without the usual bickering. I would get his share of scraps, and that would simplify everything.

When I went into combat against coyotes, coons, badgers, bobcats, and night monsters, I would know for sure that he wouldn't be there to back me up. (He never was, but I had always clung to the foolish belief that some day he might be.)

And best of all, I would be spared the tiresome ordeal of hearing about his allergies, his "stobbed ub dose," and his so-called bad leg.

In other words, Life Without Drover wouldn't be such a bad deal. I had a feeling that I could get along just fine without him.

Life Without
Drover

Once I had worked through all the pluses and minuses of Life Without Drover, I felt great. The only problem was that the good feeling lasted only two minutes, and at that point the whole thing fell to pieces.

I found myself standing face-to-face with an awful truth: I was worried sick about the little goof, and I had to go find him before he got beat up, run over, or thrown in jail.

Was I happy about this turn of events? No. It made me so mad, I wanted to bite nails and log chains. I leaped out of the pickup, fully aware that I was disobeying Slim's orders and that I was about to risk my career for someone who probably wasn't worth it.

But what's a dog to do? We're more than the sum of our particles, and even the Head of Ranch Security has feelings. I might have wished that I had invested my feelings more wisely, but I couldn't get rid of them.

Slim would be penning cattle until the auction was finished. It usually lasted until four o'clock in the afternoon. I had about three hours to find Drover and deliver him back to the pickup. If I failed . . . I didn't even want to think about it.

The moment my feet hit the ground, I began searching for tracks, and I found plenty of them— tire tracks, about ten thousand of them, coming from every direction and pressed into the dust of the parking lot.

No luck there, and it appeared that this case would yield no hard evidence. I would have to rely on what we call Speculational Analysis. Without hard evidence, I would have to make an educated guess: if I were Drover, where would I go? And the answer that flashed across the screen of my mind was "To his mother's yard."

See, we had received a tip from our secret sources that he hadn't seen his ma in a while and wanted to pay her a visit. I'm not at liberty to discuss those sources, and I'm sure you'll understand why. If our enemies ever cracked our secret codes and figured out how we gather and process information, it could be very bad.

But back to the point. I had reason to suppose that Drover had gone to visit his mother, but only a vague idea of where she lived—in a fenced yard, somewhere south of downtown. I was in the process of weighing my options when my keen eyes picked up an object of interest.

A dog was sitting under a tree near the south door of the auction barn. It wasn't Drover (wrong color and shape), but I figured he might have some information I could use.

As I drew nearer, I realized that I knew the mutt. Hey, it was Dogpound Ralph! Remember him? He was the dogcatcher's pet basset hound and lived in a special cell at the dog pound. Ralph and I had served time together when I was on Death Row and . . . well, a special bond develops between dogs who serve time together. I knew he would be thrilled to see me again.

When I approached, he was staring at the auction barn with his big, sad basset eyes, while his huge ears flapped in the breeze. "Afternoon, Ralph. What are you doing, holding down that tree so it won't blow away?"

He gave me a glance. Maybe he didn't recognize

me. "No, somebody said they were going to have a parade. I thought I'd come watch."

"This is the livestock auction. They have parades on Main Street."

"That's too far to walk."

"Oh. Well, I'll sit down and we'll watch it together." I sat down beside him and we both stared out at the parking lot. A tumbleweed clattered across the space in front of us. "Hey, this is great. There's something inspiring about a parade, isn't there?"

For a solid minute, he didn't say anything, then his mournful eyes swung around. "That ain't a parade, it's a weed."

"Well, it's a nice weed."

"Are you trying to be funny?"

"Yes, Ralph, I admit it. I thought a little humor might liven things up, but maybe I was wrong."

"Well, it ain't funny to me. I went to all the trouble to get here, and I think I missed the parade."

"You did, Ralph. They had it on Main Street about an hour ago."

"How'd you know my name?"

"I know your name because we served time together on Death Row."

He gave me a closer look. "Oh yeah, you're Texie, right?"

"I'm not Texie."

"Huh. Noodle?"

"Hey, Ralph, you and I have a long history. We went on a Fling together, remember? You taught me all sorts of bad habits and got me arrested by the dogcatcher."

"I did? Huh. It don't ring any bells."

My temper was beginning to rise. "You know, Ralph, I thought we had a special friendship, but I guess I was wrong. Sorry I bothered you. Good-bye."

I started to leave but he said, "Oh, don't get your nose out of joint. Tell me your name one more time."

"Hank the Cowdog. I'm Head of Ranch Security on a huge outfit south of town."

"Oh yeah, it's starting to come back now." A little flicker of mischief appeared in his eyes and he grinned. "You want to go on another Fling?"

"Absolutely not. I'm here on important business."

His smile faded. "Darn. I haven't done anything naughty in three months." He yawned. "What's the important business?"

"I'm on a mission to find a dog named Drover."

"Never heard of him."

"Small, short-haired, stub-tailed little mutt."

"Oh yeah, him."

"You saw him? Today?"

"I think it was today. Hold on a second." He hiked up his right hind leg and scratched his right ear. "Sorry, I had to scratch."

"I noticed."

"I've got big ears, and when they itch, boy, do they itch."

"So you saw Drover, today?"

"I guess it was him. He sat right there where you're sitting for, oh, half an hour. We missed the parade together."

"Did he talk?"

"Oh yeah, talked my ear off."

"About what? Be specific."

"Butterflies. He said he likes to chase 'em."

"It was Drover." I rose to my feet and began pacing. I could see that getting information out of Ralph wasn't going to be easy. "Ralph, I need facts and details. Did he say anything about his mother?"

"Yeah, he said he had one."

"Yes, yes? What else?"

He yawned again. "Well, I told him I had one, too."

I whirled around and stuck my nose in his face. "Ralph, I don't care about your mother. I'm working a case and you're making it very difficult."

"You're too pushy."

"Ralph, in my line of work, they don't give awards to nice guys. I'm pushy because I have to be."

"You're still too pushy."

"Too bad. Okay, you and Drover sat here and waited for a parade that didn't happen. You talked about butterflies, then he left, right? I mean, he doesn't seem to be here now."

Ralph glanced around. "I guess he did. Seemed like a nice little pooch."

"He's a nice little lunatic. Where did he go?"

"Well . . . 'scuse me a second." He hiked up his back leg and hacked at his ear again. "That thing won't leave me alone."

"Where did he go, Ralph?"

"Who?"

"Drover, the nice little lunatic who was talking about butterflies."

He stared at me for a long time. "Hey, I remember you now. You ate a bar of soap, and Jimmy Joe thought you had hydrophobia. Heh heh. Have you ate any soap lately?"

I paced a few steps away from him and looked up at the sky. I didn't want to scream at him, but he was about to drive me nuts. "Ralph, I know this is hard, but you must concentrate. Don't talk about soap or parades or your mother. Think back. When Drover left, did he say where he was going?"

Ralph scowled and rolled his eyes around. This time, at last, he seemed to be concentrating. "Yes, he did, sure did."

"Great. That's all I need to know. Where did he go?"

"Well sir, that's the part I don't remember. I think I nodded off to sleep, and next thing I knew, you showed up."

The air hissed out of my lungs as I stood there, looking down at this nincompoop of a dog. "Ralph, I have spent my whole career interrogating witnesses. Some of those interrogations were good and some were bad, but you've set a new record for . . ."

His ears shot up. "Wait. I just remembered something. He went off to the south . . . and he was follered by two bad-looking dogs."

Those words hung in the air between us. Two bad-looking dogs? Uh-oh, unless I was badly mistaken, Drover was being stalked by Buster and Muggs.

I rushed back to the spot where Ralph was sitting. "Ralph, that is very important information. Why didn't you tell me sooner?"

"Oh, didn't think of it, I guess."

"We don't have much time. If those two thugs get hold of him . . ."

All at once my nostrils picked up the smell of steak fumes. What are steak fumes? They're the odor, the powerful odor that fills the air when somebody is cooking steaks on an outdoor grill.

Steak Fumity is one of several forces in the universe that are very predictable. Gravity causes a rubber ball to fall to the earth. Ungravity causes it to bounce back toward the moon, and Steak Fumity will snap a dog's head around and get his attention. These forces never change, and we even have mathematical equations that describe them. You want to take a peek at our equation for Steak Fumity? Okay, pay attention. We don't have all day.

$$S + Fr \times 2(HD) = Fm + SL$$

Pretty impressive, huh? You bet. Do we need to go over the terms and explain them in everyday language? Maybe so. Okay, S is the mathematical symbol for Steak, and Fr means fire. HD is Hungry Dog, and when we multiply it by two, it doubles the value, making it Very Hungry Dog. Fm stands for Fumes, and SL is the scientific term for Steak Lust.

So there you have it: *Steak plus Fire times Very Hungry Dog equals Fumes plus Steak Lust.* See, that wasn't so bad, was it? I get a kick out of playing around with Heavy Duty Mathematics. Most of your ordinary mutts sit around scratching fleas and figuring out new ways of saying "Duh." Me? In my spare moments, I'm doing algebra and clackulus.

Anyway, my nostrils were picking up powerful waves of Steak Fumity and fellers, those smells will focus a dog's mind—not once in a while but every time. My body turned like the needle in a haystack . . . the needle on a compass, let us say, toward a plume of smoke about fifty yards away.

In a low voice, I murmured, "Ralph, this case has taken a new direction. Someone is broiling steaks over there, and we need to check it out."

And as if by magic, my feet began carrying the rest of me toward the source of the delicious fumes.

A Cowboy
Cook

~~~~~~

See, the livestock auction had a little café, and every Wednesday during the sale, they served lunch. I'd heard Slim talking about their home-made cherry pie. As I recall, what he said was "It's even better than mine." I think that was some kind of joke, since he'd never made a pie in his whole life, and if he ever did, nobody would eat it. I sure wouldn't.

The café also served burgers and steaks, and it appeared that someone was cooking them on an outdoor barbecue grill near the back door of the café. That was the source of the steak fumes and that's where my legs were taking me, straight toward the cloud of white smoke that combined the delicious smells of mesquite coals and broiling meat.

Sniff sniff slurp.

Fifty feet away, my mouth began to water as my mind projected pictures of hunks of beef hissing over a bed of glowing mesquite coals. The pictures were so vivid, I tried to snatch one of the steaks, but, well, pretty pictures in the mind are pretty empty and a guy finds himself biting thin air, is what happens. That's not the sort of thing you want to do in public, go around trying to snap steak-mirages out of the air.

Dogpound Ralph was following me, and he noticed. "What did you have in mind?"

"I have steak in mind, Ralph. I plan to beg or borrow a steak. That's what we did when you and I went on The Fling, remember?"

"Yeah, but you messed it up and got caught."

"A plate fell off the grill and broke. It was an accident. It could have happened to anyone."

He trotted up beside me. "You've got no charm or technique, just blunder in and start grabbing. Better let me handle this."

I laughed. "You? That's funny, pal, and the answer is no." I stopped and looked him straight in the eyes. "You wait right here and watch. I'll show you charm and technique. In five minutes, I'll be back with a steak."

He shrugged. "Bet you won't."

I didn't bother to argue with him. What did he know, this jailbird-dog who hung out with the local dogcatcher? I left him there and crept toward the clouds of smoke that were causing various parts of my body to do peculiar things: nose, ears, eyes, heart, lungs, and liver, every part of a dog's body that responds to delicious smells.

The trouble with these steak deals is that they're always supervised, and this one was no exception. The cook was sitting in a metal folding chair, his left boot resting on his knee, and right away I picked up a couple of clues that told me that he was wearing a Cowboy Cook Costume.

First, he wore his pant legs tucked inside the tops of his boots. Second, his jeans were hitched up with a pair of bright red suspenders. Third, he wore a huge bushy mustache that was waxed on the ends, and fourth, he wore a big cowboy hat with a wide brim and a tall crown.

See, your ordinary everyday cowboy or rancher (Slim and Loper, for example) wouldn't dress in such a gaudy fashion, but a guy who'd been hired as a cowboy cook *would*. A lot of dogs wouldn't have noticed such tiny details, but I picked 'em up right away. Oh, and I almost forgot the fifth clue: that big hat had no sweat stains around the base of the crown.

Heh heh. These guys can't get up early enough in the morning to fool Hank the Cowdog. He wasn't a working cowboy. They'd hired him as a cook.

He'd dug a fire pit in the ground, burned a batch of mesquite wood down to coals, and had laid an iron grill across the pit. Steaks and burgers hissed on the grill, and nearby he had a big cast-iron pot hanging over the fire.

As I approached his camp, I slowed my pace. I mean, I didn't want him to get the wrong idea, that I was just some mutt who'd come to poach a steak or something like that. Cowboy chefs are pretty suspicious of dogs who come up to watch them cook, don't you know, so I made it appear that I had . . . well, stumbled upon his camp by accident. No fevered eyes, no dripping chops, no frenzied tail-wags.

He looked up and saw me, and for a moment I wasn't sure which way this would go, whether he would leap out of his chair and yell at me, or invite me to, uh, share his campfire. He had a pair of friendly eyes, and after a bit, he smiled beneath his mustache and said, "Hello, pup. Pull up a chair. You want a cup of coffee?"

I think that was a joke. Dogs don't drink coffee or sit in chairs, but his manner was cordial, so I went to him and sat down beside his chair. He scratched me behind the ears and gave me a pat on the ribs. This was a nice man, and obviously he liked . . . sniff, sniff . . . dogs. This deal appeared to be moving in the right direction.

He cocked his head back and looked me over. "Well, you've got some tallow on your ribs, so I guess you're not a stray."

Oh no, not a stray. I had a steady job on a steak . . . on a ranch, that is. I thumped my tail on the ground to add some sincerity to my, uh, presentation.

"Don't be stirring up the dust."

Oh, the tail, sorry.

"Mrs. Berry don't approve of sand on the meat."

Right, no problem. I flipped two switches and shut down the tail.

He leaned back in his chair and took a deep breath. "Steaks sure smell good, don't they?"

Steaks? What steaks? Oh, by George, he had some steaks on the grill! Ha ha. I hadn't even noticed.

"Those are rib-eyes, pup, USDA Grade Awesome." He pushed himself up out of his chair. "Say, I need to step inside for just a second. Would you keep your eye on them steaks for me?"

Slurp. Oh sure, anything for a friend.

"I won't be long."

Heh heh. Neither would I.

The instant I heard the screen door close behind him, I whipped my head around to the grill and stared at the steaks, twenty of them, and I can hardly describe the emotions that were bouncing off the walls of my mind.

Never in my wildest dreams would I have thought that this job would turn out to be so easy. I mean, cowboys *know* dogs, and as a general rule, you can expect that they have a pretty good understanding of . . . well, the temptations that we face every day. Yet this guy—I didn't even know his name—this cowboy cook had walked off and left ME in charge of twenty sizzling rib-eye steaks!

Holy smokes, this was Christmas for Dogs! A river was running through my mouth. I was shaking with excitement, my heart was racing, my eyes were fluttering, and I took a creeping step toward . . .

"That's what I figured."

Huh? A voice had come out of nowhere and froze me in my tracks. An instant later, the screen door opened and out came my, uh, new friend, the cowboy cook. His mouth held an odd, lopsided smile. He sat down in his chair and said, "Come here." I rushed over to him and laid my head in his lap and went to Slow Thumps on the tail section.

"Don't stir up the dust."

Oh yes, sorry.

He took my face in his hands and looked into my eyes. "Let me tell you a little story." He reached down and flipped up the lid of a . . . what was that? Oh, it was a guitar case, and he pulled out a guitar. And he started singing this song.

Ed and the Cheese

At fifty a bachelor cowboy named Ed
Took a job on a ranch on a fork of the Red.
He wintered that year by himself in a shack
With a leaky old roof and a privy out back.
He had him a cook stove, a chest, and a bed.
The place wasn't fancy but neither was Ed.
But then he took notice of something not right.
He had him a roommate that came out at night.
Ed never did see him but knew he was there,
From the mess on the cabinet and
a hole in the chair.
So Ed, he decided to give it a test,
Left two hunks of cheese in plain sight
on the chest.
Next morning he checked it and
sure 'nuff he found
His roommate had snuck out

and gobbled it down.

Ed nodded and gave his two fingers a snap

And left his new buddy some cheese in a trap.

This tale has a moral for those who will hear.

There's danger in being a rat with no fear.

Old Ed lured him out and caught him with ease,

'Cause a thief can't resist taking

unguarded cheese.

The cowboy placed his guitar back in its case and turned his eyes on me. "So there it is, pup. Did you get the point?"

The point? Well, it wasn't a bad song (I'd heard worse from Slim Chance), but I hadn't noticed anything especially pointy about it. No.

He leaned back in his chair and parked one leg over the opposite knee. "See, when I stepped into the café, I was giving you a test."

A test?

"And you flunked. You ain't exactly a thief, but only because I didn't give you the chance."

I hardly knew what to say. What a cheap trick!

"The point is, you told me what was on your mind."

Well, what did he expect? Hey, I wasn't Mister Perfect Doggie. What kind of dog would sit there and ignore twenty hissing steaks on the grill?

He gave me a grin. "It was nice knowing you, but now you have to move along." He brought his face right down to my nose and narrowed his eyes. "'Cause we ain't feeding steaks to the dogs today."

Fine! I didn't want his old steaks anyway. The very idea, him pulling sneaky tricks on a dog who'd come over to pay a friendly visit! I'd never been so insulted. I lifted my head to a proud angle and marched away. This was outrageous!

Furthermore, I had important work to do. A friend of mine, who happened to be an incredible ninny, was running loose in town, and I had to find him before he . . .

"Hey, pooch, I might let you taste my beans. You like cowboy beans?"

No, I did not like cowboy beans, especially if they were made by a sneak who laid traps for innocent dogs. We dogs have our pride, and just because we get hungry once in a while doesn't mean . . . on the other hand, a guy should never let pride rule his roost.

I, uh, did an about-face and went back to the fire and gave him an expression that said, "Okay, as a personal favor, I'll try your beans."

He lifted the lid on the big cast-iron pot and dipped out some beans into a tin plate. "It's a new recipe. I call it 'Gasping Delight.'"

Interesting name. Hurry up.

"Now, it's got a few peppers in it . . ." He set the plate on the ground in front of me. ". . . so you might want to eat it kind of slow."

Never tell a dog how to eat. We invented eating.

I put my nose into the plate and started wolfing like there was no tomorrow. Good. Real good. Hey, these were some very tasty beans. Too bad I lived with cowboys who weren't smart enough to make a pot of . . .

All at once, my eyes began to water and something strange was going on inside my mouth. HARK! GASP! *What was that stuff?*

"Reckon I made 'em a little too hot?"

I stared at him through swimming eyes. "A little too hot? Buddy, somebody dumped a sack of gunpowder into your stupid beans and you don't need to worry about *me* hanging around. Good-bye!"

And with that, I whirled around and stormed away. Hark.

CHAPTER NINE

Back on the Case

It worked out fine. I didn't have time to waste on cowboy cooks or nitro-beans, because I was on an important mission. Had you forgotten about Drover? Well, maybe I had too, but a three-alarm fire in my mouth brought me crashing back to reality.

Ralph was sitting in the same spot where I'd left him, only now he wore a wicked little grin. "Told you."

"Ralph, you can shut your trap any time you wish."

"You've got no charm or technique. Your face is a flashing neon sign."

"Ralph, he used trickery. He cheated, but never

mind. I'm on a mission to save my friend. You said he went north?"

"South."

"I'm almost sure you said north."

He rolled his eyes. "I said *south*. It rhymes with Ralph, and maybe I'd better go with you."

"You're too slow."

He pushed himself up from the ground. "I'm slow, but I know the difference between north and south." He gave me a wink. "Three."

"I don't understand that."

"Well, it was a joke, and it went past you like a fast ball. Let's go." He waddled off to the south.

"Don't give me orders, Ralph. And don't forget who's in charge." I hurried and caught up with him. "Explain your joke."

"If you subtract north from south, the answer is three."

"It makes no sense."

"It's a joke."

"Ralph, it's not funny. You're in over your head."

"His name was Corky."

"What?"

"I just remembered your buddy's name. It was Corky and he's a Yorkie."

I laughed. "That's not bad. You're getting better."

"It wasn't a joke."

"With you, it's hard to tell, isn't it? When we wrap up this case, I'll give you a few tips on humor."

"Meathead."

"Yes, those were some beautiful steaks. Too bad I didn't get one."

"There's a lot you don't get."

"Exactly. But you know, Ralph, life goes on in spite of our little setbacks."

"His name was Corky."

"Yeah? Well, don't try his beans. They'd take the paint off a barn."

"You're looking for the wrong dog."

"I agree. He's not worth it, but he's my friend and I'm . . . I wish you wouldn't roll your eyes when I'm talking. It's very rude."

"Just skip it."

That ended the conversation, which was fine with me. To be honest, I found it hard to communicate with Ralph, and his jokes were really bad. That came as no surprise because . . . well, the guy was a basset hound and what can you expect? If my face was a neon sign advertising Steak Lust, his was a billboard that blared the message "I have no sense of humor."

He had zero sense of humor, but maybe he could help me find Drover.

We headed south on a course that took us back to Main Street and the center of town. You've seen pictures of downtown Dallas and New York City, right? Well, downtown Twitchell was about the same: a drugstore, Leonard's Saddle Shop, the pool hall, a couple of clothing stores, a grocery store, and Twitchell Hardware. Huge place. A dog could get lost without even trying, especially if his name was Drover.

When we reached downtown, I did a thorough Recon of the whole area. I sure didn't want to walk into some kind of disaster. Don't forget that Twitchell had a dogcatcher and two stray dogs named Buster and Muggs, to whom I had recently, uh, mouthed off. I had no wish to run into any of them.

The street that had been lined with cheering crowds only hours before was now fairly empty and quiet, with just the normal flow of cars and pickups, and an occasional cattle truck riding its jake-brake through town. (Big diesel trucks have this thing called a jake-brake that makes the engine roar, and truck drivers love using it when they pass through a town.)

There wasn't much action in downtown Twitchell, so Ralph and I picked up the pace and headed south. Or let's put it this way: I tried to pick up the pace, but Ralph had trouble keeping up. Not only did he have short legs, but he couldn't seem to walk fifty feet without stepping on his ears.

By the time we had come to a residential neighborhood south of the downtown area, Ralph was out of breath. "Hey, can we stop and rest?"

I came to a stop. "Okay, two minutes. We haven't a moment to lose."

"If you're in such a hurry, how come you took time to steal a steak?"

I beamed him a glare. "I had no intention of stealing a steak. My plan from the beginning was to coax one out of the cook."

"Well, he sure got the wrong impression, since he sang you that song about the rat and the cheese."

"A dog in my position deals with larger concepts, Ralph. I'm not responsible for wrong impressions. Are you ready to move out?"

"Just another minute. How are you going to find Corky's mother?"

"I have a plan, and that's all you need to know. And, for the last time, his name is Drover."

"He told me it was Corky Yorkie."

"Ralph, you need to get your ears fixed. You've

87

stepped on them so many times, it's damaged your hearing. Are you rested up?"

"Not quite."

"Good, let's move out."

You know, Ralph was a nice guy and we'd had a few laughs together, but he could be really tiresome. I guess that's what happens to a dog that spends most of his time riding around town in the back of the dogcatcher's pickup.

But the important thing was that Ralph wasn't leading this mission. I was, and I had devised a clever plan for finding the yard where Drover's mother stayed . . . the poor woman.

You want to hear my plan? Okay, here we go. We walked up and down the alleys and I called out, "May I have your attention please? Will Drover's mother please report to the front?"

Pretty awesome plan, huh? You bet. Simple but effective, and I had a feeling that it would work like a cork . . . like a charm, let us say.

As you can see, Ralph's blabbering had taken its toll. How else can you explain that a word like "cork" would pop up in my thoughts? It just goes to prove . . . all at once I can't remember what it proves, but it proves something very important and we should never forget it.

Where were we? Oh yes, executing my plan. Ralph and I walked down alleys, calling for Drover's mother to step forward and identify herself. After an hour, we'd had no success and I began to wonder if the poor woman had gone into hiding. Maybe she didn't want to admit her part in producing a little mutt like Drover. I couldn't blame her, but it did nothing to ease my mind. With every passing minute, my concern about his safety grew deeper and darker.

And don't forget that I was operating under a deadline. When the sale ended at the auction barn, Slim would load his horse and head back to the ranch. I sure as thunder didn't want to miss the bus.

I was about ready to abandon the mission, when it happened. As I recall, we were in the third alley west of Main Street and that's when we heard a voice. It said, and this is a direct quote, it said, "Yeah, that's me. Who wants to know?"

I called back, "Hank the Cowdog. I'm with Search and Rescue. We're looking for your son." I turned to Ralph with a triumphant smile. "At last, we've found her!"

Ralph shook his head. "Voice is too deep."

"Ralph, some mothers have deeper voices than others. They can't help it."

"I'm telling you, that ain't a mother's voice."

"What do you know about it? Have you ever been a mother?"

"Nope, but I had one and she didn't sound like that."

"Congratulations. You get three points for having a mother. Now hush." I turned back toward the place from whence the voice had come. "Hello again? Madame, we're wondering if you've seen Drover."

There was a moment of silence, then the voice replied, "No, we ain't seen Drover, but we see you! Har har."

A buzz of electrical current shot down my spine, and I felt the hair rising on the back of my neck. I turned to Ralph. "That's a deep voice. It doesn't sound like a mother, does it?"

Ralph rolled his eyes. "Meathead."

"Stop calling me names! I'm getting a bad feeling about this."

"You ought to."

"And do you know why? That voice reminds me of someone I've met before and never want to meet again."

At that very moment, two big scruffy dogs stepped out from behind a shrub. I heard the air rushing into my chest and felt my eyes bugging out. Are you ready for some shocking news? Hang on.

It was Buster and Muggs. Pretty scary, huh? You bet, and you'll be sorry to hear that it got worse.

CHAPTER TEN

We Get
Ambushed

So there we were, Ralph and I, trapped in an alley with Buster and Muggs, two of the toughest dogs in Ochiltree County.

You might recall that Muggs was a heavyset bulldog-type of mutt with an overbite in his lower jaw. He was rolling the muscles in his thick shoulders and looked as though he was ready to go ten rounds with anyone unfortunate enough to get caught in the ring with him.

"We got 'im, boss! It's the jerk that was running his mouth at the parade."

Buster was a nondescript mixed breed, taller than Muggs but not as heavily muscled. He held me in a hard gaze and gave a chuckle that froze my blood. "Yeah, we've got him in a back alley, and there ain't no way out."

"What should we do, boss, huh, huh? You want that I should jump him and, you know, give him a treatment? Har har." Before Buster could answer, Muggs turned to me. "We seen you making stupid faces at us, jerk, and that made us really mad, oh yeah." He turned back to Buster. "What do you tink, boss? Huh, huh? Reckon it's time to do some work on his face?"

Buster held up a paw for silence. "Easy, Muggsie. Don't forget, he's Head of Ranch Security."

"Yeah, I'll show him some ranch security! Just tell me when."

Buster walked over to me and pointed toward Muggs. "You know, pal, he don't like you. I mean, down deep he's a very tender guy, but when you stuck out your tongue, it done something to his . . . whatever you call it. His spirit. It's like you drove a stake clean through his heart."

Muggs was beginning to foam at the mouth. "Yeah, and I'm fixing to make a steak out of him, too!"

Buster looked me up and down. "Let me tell you something, pal. Out on the ranch, maybe you're hot stuff, but when you come to town, you're just another mutt. See, we *own* this town."

Muggs growled, "Yeah, and we ain't selling to you, jerk, are we, boss?"

"That's right, Muggsie." Back to me. "So maybe you'd like to apologize to my friend, huh?"

I swallowed hard and tried to hide the quiver in my voice. "I had no idea he was so sensitive."

"Yeah, but are you sorry you hurt his feelings? I mean, you really wounded him."

"I'm sorry."

"Louder, and say it to Muggsie."

"Muggs, I'm sorry I stuck out my tongue at you."

Buster smiled. "There it is, Muggsie. He said he was sorry. Do you think he's really sorry or just saying it 'cause he's chicken?"

Muggs's eyes were flaming. "Oh, I tink he's chicken, boss, and I love drumsticks, oh yeah!"

Buster gave me a shrug. "That's what I figured. Muggsie's terrible to hold a grudge. I fear I can't hold him back." His eyes drifted over to Ralph. He'd been sitting like a statue and hadn't moved a hair. "What's that?"

"That's Ralph."

"If I had ears that big, I'd rent 'em out for a circus tent. What is he, some kind of hound dog?"

"He's a basset."

"No kidding?" Buster shot a grin at Muggs.

"Say Muggsie, you ever whip a basset hound?"

"Oh yeah, boss, they're easy. Just turn me loose."

"Be patient, Muggsie, I'm having fun." Buster turned back to me. "Does Ralph talk or just sit there?" He waved a paw in front of Ralph's glazed eyes. "Hey, you with the big ears. You got something to say?"

After a moment of silence, Ralph said, "The dogcatcher's having coffee at the Dixie Dog."

Buster stared at him. "Oh yeah? Well, I guess that's good to know, 'cause he ain't no friend of ours. But deep in my heart, Ralph, I'm wondering . . . so what?"

Ralph said, "Make a run for the Dixie Dog."

Buster and Muggs exchanged glances and laughed. Buster said, "Now wait a second, Ralph. That don't make sense. See, Muggsie and me have a reputation in this town. The dogcatcher would love to haul us to the pound, right, Muggs?"

Muggs was on his hind legs, throwing punches in the air. "Yeah, only he can't catch us, har har."

All at once, I noticed that Ralph was doing funny things with his eyes, rolling them around. He had done it several times that afternoon, but this time . . . well, his eyes seemed to be pointing toward the north. And unless I was mistaken, he appeared to be gesturing . . . well, to me. But why would he be doing that?

Then it hit me. *He wasn't talking to Buster— he was talking to me!* Don't you get it? Ralph was the dogcatcher's pet, and if we made a dash to the Dixie Dog Drive-in . . .

My mind was racing. Somehow we had to break out of this trap and make a run for it. But how?

What saved us was that I happened to notice a tiny detail that most dogs would have missed. A cat was sitting on the fence only ten feet away from where we were standing. She'd been sunning herself and purring and watching the show in the alley. And all at once a plan took shape in my mind.

In a calm voice, I said, "Hey Muggs, did you hear what that cat just said?"

Muggs stopped throwing punches and jerked his head from side to side. "Naw, what cat?"

I pointed to the fence. "She said that if you want to lose a few ugly pounds, you should cut off your head."

His eyes grew wide. "A cat said that?"

"That's what I heard."

"Oh man, she shouldn't ought to have said that. No cat says stuff like that to Muggsie and gets away with it." He puffed himself up and stomped over to the fence. "Hey dummy, I said what you just heard . . . I heard what you just said, and you're in deep trouble, oh yeah!"

The cat didn't move or flinch or twitch, just sat there purring and staring down at Muggs. She knew she was safe on the fence and wasn't the least bit concerned about his threats.

That just made him madder. He started bouncing up and down and foaming at the mouth, and I think his eyes even crossed. Buster watched with a sour expression and growled, "Skip it, Muggsie, we've got better things to do."

But Muggs had moved beyond hearing. He leaped up on his hind legs and placed his front paws on the fence. Then, stretching his thick body as far as it would stretch, he placed his nose and fanged mouth only inches away from the cat.

"You hair-puff jerk of a cat, I'm fixing to fix you!"

At this point in the drama, two things happened. First, Ralph began backing away, and second, the cat's paw struck like a snake. BAM! I mean, it came out of nowhere and nailed Muggs on the nose.

And Muggs lost what little mind he had left. We're talking about insane. He barked, he growled, he snapped, he slobbered, he lunged, and every

time his nose came within six inches of the cat, she gave him a whack.

As you know, I have no use for a cat, but I must admit that this one was a piece of work. She was like a little machine: serene, poised, quiet, and very efficient. Bark *whack*, bark *whack*, bark *whack*! I mean, she didn't hiss or growl, just sat there taking his nose apart, and old Muggsie kept going back for more of that home cookin'.

I would have enjoyed staying for the whole show, but while Buster and Muggs were occupied, I followed Ralph's lead and began oozing down the alley to the north, then turned and ran like a streak of greased lightning.

Behind me, I heard Buster growl at Muggs, "Hey, genius, you'd better quit while you've got a nose left!"

At the end of the block, I came out of the alley and hooked a sharp turn to the right, spun all four paws on the pavement, and set sail for Main Street. On Main, I hooked a left and went zooming up the street. There, about fifty yards south of the Dixie Dog Drive-in, I caught up with Ralph, who was running just as fast as his stubby legs would take him.

By now, I could see the dogcatcher's pickup parked in front of the Dixie Dog, a white Ford with the CITY OF TWITCHELL sign on the doors and the dog cage in the back. At last I began to relax a little bit.

"Nice work, Ralph. I think we've got it made."

"We ain't there yet."

Then it happened. He stepped on one of his ears and wrecked his little basset body all over the sidewalk. He rolled ten times and came to a stop when he hit a trash receptacle.

I wasn't particularly worried until I heard barking dogs in the distance . . . and saw Buster and Muggs come ripping up the street toward us.

"Get up, son, the posse's on our trail!"

"I hurt my toe."

"Don't tell me about your toe. Those guys want our heads! Run!"

He ran, or tried to run. Have you ever watched a basset hound run? The best of them can sprint about as fast as a worm or a turtle. I'm talking slow.

He chugged along, and I could hear Buster and Muggs coming up fast, closing the lead we'd enjoyed up to that point. And fellers, let me tell you, it was spooky. Behind me, I could hear them making all kinds of awful sounds: rumbling, snorting, snapping their teeth, and growling about all the hideous things they were going to do to us.

I was starting to worry about this deal. How can you lose a race when you had a lead of a hundred yards? With Ralph, it was easy.

"Hey, Ralph, what do we do when we get to the Dixie Dog?"

"Well, I hadn't thought that far ahead."

"Start thinking about it. They're closing the gap." At last we made it to the dogcatcher's pickup, and the thugs were coming hard and fast. "Okay, pal, what now?"

He gave me a wink. "I think I've got it figgered." He chugged around to the back of the pickup, where the cage stood empty. The door of the cage wasn't latched, and Ralph nosed it open. "Come on, we'll hop inside the cage."

Inside the dogcatcher's cage? That didn't sound like a great idea, but I didn't have a better one. Ralph went into a deep crouch and sprang upward. I watched, amazed, as he scratched and scrambled, trying to make it inside the cage . . . and rolled back down on the street.

"Ralph, for crying out loud, hurry up!"

Again, he crouched and lunged and . . . I couldn't believe it! He came rolling back out. By that time, there was no chance that we could both make it into the cage, and I had to make a quick decision: run or fight.

If I ran, they would get Ralph. If I fought them off, maybe Ralph could scramble into the cage, and at least one of us would survive to tell the story.

This has gotten pretty scary, hasn't it? I tried to warn you. Don't continue reading unless you're pretty tough.

CHAPTER ELEVEN

Caution: Really Scary Stuff

If I'd had more time to weigh the options and consider the consequences, I might have come to a different decision, but we were out of time. Buster and Muggs had arrived, and someone had to do something. Ralph was worthless, so that left me to deal with the problem.

I wouldn't call it a heroic decision. It was the sort of thing any decent dog would have done. If you're worth more than an ordinary rock, you help your friends. If you don't, you're a rat.

I turned to the villains with a calm smile, and . . . yipes. I can't describe the level of nastiness I saw in their faces. They were beyond mad and had tumbled into some dark zone where things get crunched and torn.

Buster blistered me with an evil glare. "Wise guy, huh? Thought you could make us look ridiculous, huh?"

Muggs had foam dripping off his tusks, and his eyes were clouded with rage. "Oh, you're going to get it now, jerk, oh yeah! Everyting that cat gave me, I'm going to give back to you, only ten times worser!"

"That's right, cowdog. See, we don't appreciate getting conned in our own town."

"That's right, jerk!"

"It's embarrassing, if you know what I mean."

"Yeah, and we're so mean, you can't even spell how mean we are, jerk!"

Buster lifted his right paw as though it were a sledgehammer and admired it. "Which of us shall take the first shift, Muggsie?"

Muggs bounced up and down, a bomb that was aching to explode. "Oh, that's easy, boss. I'll go first, only there ain't going to be any second, 'cause when I get done, there won't even be a greasy spot left on the pavement, oh yeah!"

"Well?" Buster gave me a smirk. "It was nice knowing you, cowdog. Git 'im, Muggs, git 'im!"

Muggs came at me like a train. I braced myself on all four legs and gave him my best shot. You ever give your best shot to a train? When I stopped rolling, Muggs was all over me—fangs, claws, clubs, and paws, snaps and snarls and bloody threats. I rolled up into a ball and tried to protect my throat, but I knew it was only a matter of time until . . .

But then, the most amazing thing happened. All at once, Muggs was gone. He just vanished, evaporated. I was lying in the parking lot of the Dixie Dog Drive-in, blinking my eyes and wondering what had happened.

I sat up and glanced around and saw . . . Jimmy Joe Dogcatcher. He was holding a dip-net and glaring off into the distance. Ralph was sitting inside the cage, his eyes as big as custard pies.

Jimmy Joe muttered, "Dadgum dogs! One of these days, I'll get 'em snared. Are you hurt, Ralphie?"

Ralph sat there, moon-eyed, and thumped his tail. I got the impression that he didn't know if he was hurt or not. I could have told him: he wasn't hurt.

The dogcatcher turned a scowl on me. "Well, hop into the cage. I'll give you a ride."

Out of the corner of my eye, I half-noticed that Ralph seemed to be shaking his head. Unfortunately, I didn't give it much thought. I hopped into the cage, and Jimmy Joe closed the door behind me. He climbed into the pickup and we headed south down Main Street.

Ralph gave me a mournful look. "Well, you've done it now."

"Done what?"

"Well, you jumped right into a trap."

"I don't know what you mean."

"You're in the dogcatcher's cage."

"Well, sure, but he offered to give me a ride."

Ralph leaned toward me. "To the dog pound."

"What? You mean . . ."

"He's the dogcatcher. He catches dogs; only he didn't even have to catch you."

"What! Why, this is an outrage! I demand . . . hey, Ralph, I hope this is another one of your jokes."

"Meathead."

"So . . . it's not a joke?"

"Double-meathead."

Well, that killed the conversation. We rode in eerie silence down Main Street, the same street where, in happier times, the citizens of Twitchell had turned out in droves and honored me with a parade. It was all a hollow memory now. Nobody stood on the curbs to cheer me as I made the silent journey to Devil's Island for Dogs.

At the south end of town, we made a left turn

onto a dusty road that led to the city dog pound, a collection of depressing sheds and cages where unlucky dogs came to wait for the wheels of justice to do their grim work.

As we neared the pound, I found myself looking at the skeleton of a dead tree, filled with ten head of grinning buzzards. It wasn't what you would call a happy omen, and it would have caused my spirits to sink if they hadn't already sunk.

We pulled up beside the prison compound and stopped. Jimmy Joe got out, opened the cage door, and slipped a noose around my neck. I figured we were going to attend a hanging, but he led me to a cell and left me inside.

He closed the door and looked down at me. "Well, I didn't get the ones I wanted, but I got you." He leaned down toward me and whispered, "Don't ever hitch a ride with the dogcatcher. It'll come back to bite you every time."

On a better day, I might have thought of some snappy reply, but a cloud of gloom had settled over me and I couldn't think of anything snappy to say. Actually, he had given me some good advice: "Don't ever hitch a ride with the dogcatcher." Too bad I hadn't thought of it myself.

For better or worse, Ralph hung around to keep me company. As Jimmy Joe's personal pet,

he had free run of the place and sat outside my cell, while Jimmy Joe did his chores, putting out feed and water for the prisoners.

I wasn't in the mood for conversation, but after a while, Ralph said, "That was pretty shrewd, what you done with the cat. You sure fooled 'em."

"Yes, and a lot of good it did."

Ralph began scratching his ear. "Boy, that cat really cleaned Muggsie's plow. I hated to leave, it was so much fun to watch. Oh, and thanks for fighting them dogs and letting me hop in the cage. They would have eaten me alive."

"Yeah, well, they did a pretty good job on me." I rose to my feet and began pacing around my cell. "But you know, Ralph, the saddest part of this is that I failed in my primary mission. We never found my friend Drover."

Ralph sat there for a moment, staring off into the distance. Then he said, "I'm going to tell you this one more time." He gave me a hard look. "The dog I was talking to at the sale barn was named CORKY."

"What? But you said . . ."

"His name was Corky, and he was a Yorkie. I never saw your pal Drover."

"What! Then where did he go?"

"Well, I don't know. If he's wandering around town, Jimmy Joe'll scoop him up and he'll end up out here with you."

I marched over to Ralph and glared at him through the fence. "Ralph, you had two hours to give me that information. Why didn't you?"

He heaved a sigh and shook his head. "Because you're a meathead. You're kind of a nice meathead, but I've met stumps that listen better than you do."

Those words tumbled through my mind, and I heard myself uttering a bitter laugh. "So here I am, locked in a prison cell, and Drover is wandering around, lost in space . . . and it was all for nothing." I took a deep breath. "Ralph, what would you think if I sang you a song?"

He gave me a blank stare. "Sang me a song? Why would you do that?"

"Because . . . because there are times when only music can express the incredible gloom that fills our souls."

He shrugged. "Sure. I ain't got anything better to do."

And so, right then and there, I sang him this song about the tragedy my life had become. Check it out. . . .

The Low-down Dogpound Blues

Once upon a time, I was proud and free,
In charge of Ranch Security.
At the height of my maturity,
I went to town.
Caught a ride in the back of a pickup truck.
Had a grand old time until my luck
Had a cardiac arrest, and now I'm stuck
In the pound.
I've got the Low-down Dogpound Blues,
There's nothing more to lose.
The trouble was I didn't think
I could end up in the clink.
I guess I should have tried to hide
When Jimmy Joe offered me a ride,
But like a fool, I jumped inside
The cage, in his truck.
I thought the man was being kind
And didn't want me left behind.
But now I think I lost my mind.
Never ride with the dogcatcher.
I've got the Low-down Dogpound Blues,
There's nothing more to lose.
The trouble was I didn't think
I could end up in the clink.
I'm sure my mother never thought

The puppy that she raised and taught
Would go astray and have to rot
In a jail in Twitchell.
But here I am, down at the mouth.
My luck ran out, my life went south.
I'm doing time with Dogpound Ralph
In a prison for dogs.
I've got the Low-down Dogpound Blues,
There's nothing more to lose.
The trouble was I didn't think
I could end up in the clink.
I've got the Low-down Dogpound Blues.
I'm sad down to my shoes.
The problem was . . .
The problem was, I didn't *think*.

Drover Is Lost Forever

Pretty sad song, huh? You bet. I mean, for a few precious moments, Ralph and I were the only two dogs in the whole world, and I opened the floodgates of my emotions and let 'em come pouring out.

I was shocked when I looked up and saw that my prison buddy had fallen asleep. "Hey, wake up! For crying out loud, I just poured out my heart and soul, and you couldn't even stay awake for it!"

He flinched and opened his eyes. That was a pretty depressing sight in itself, the sad eyes of a basset hound. He stared at me for a moment and said, "His name was Corky."

"We've already discussed that, Ralph. I made a

tragic mistake, and you stood by and let me ruin my life, but the point is that you fell asleep in the middle of my song."

He yawned. "Was it pretty good?"

"It was a great song. I'm just sorry I wasted it on you. Furthermore . . ."

He gave me a pained look and held up one paw. "Shhh, not so loud. You're hurting my ears."

That drove me deeper into anger. "You're worried about your ears? Ralph, I'm rotting away in prison. I've lost my home, my career, and all my friends. I'm left here with *you*, and you can't even stay awake!"

He brought a paw to his lips. "Shhhhhh."

"Don't shush me, you flop-eared donkey of a dog! If I ever get out of here . . ."

He leaned toward me and muttered, "You probably will, if you'll be patient and shut your big mouth."

He jerked his head toward . . . I turned my gaze in the direction his nose was pointing, and saw that Jimmy Joe had finished his chores. He washed his hands with a water hose, waved at Ralph, and said, "Abyssinia." Then he climbed into his pickup and drove away.

I turned to Ralph. "He's going to Abyssinia?"

"Nope. It's his way of saying, 'I'll be seeing you.' It's a little joke between us, I guess you'd say."

"Well, forgive me if I don't laugh."

He shrugged. "That's okay. If I was on Death Row, I wouldn't laugh either."

"Thanks for all your care and compassion. Now, if you'll excuse me," I began pacing around my cell, looking for any weakness that might allow me to escape, "I've got to find a way of busting out of here."

"There's a way . . . but you won't find it."

I stopped in my tracks and turned my gaze around to Ralph. "What did you say?"

He didn't answer. Instead he walked a few steps away and looked off to the north, to be sure that Jimmy Joe had gone. When he came back, the claws on his feet were clicking on the cement. "He's gone. You still want to bust out?"

"Of course I do!"

The angry tone in my voice caused him to flinch. "You make more noise than any dog I ever met. Move the dog feeder."

He pointed toward a metal object inside my cell, a box that held maybe twenty pounds of dog food kernels. It appeared to be a self-feeder, and, to be honest, I hadn't even noticed it before now.

"Ralph, did you say . . . move the feeder?"

He heaved a sigh. "Move the feeder. It's covering up a hole in the fence."

"No kidding?" I walked over to the feeder and gave it a nudge. Sure enough, it was covering a decent-sized hole in the fencing. "Hey Ralph, there's a hole in the fence. How can that be?"

"Well, the other night a raccoon showed up. He wanted the feed and tore up the fence. Big rascal, and he ate all the feed too. Jimmy Joe parked the feeder over the hole. I guess he figured most dogs would be too dumb to notice."

Our eyes met, and for a moment of heartbeats I thought of asking exactly what he meant by that, but there wasn't time. This was my chance to break out of prison, and I had to seize the sneeze before the iron got too hot.

Jimmy Joe had filled the feeder and it was heavy, but my desperate situation had given me sources of strength I didn't even know I had. After several minutes of pushing and tugging, I moved the feeder out of the way and slithered through the hole in the fence.

Safe on the other side of the prison walls, I filled my lungs with the fresh air of freedom and gave a triumphant shout. Then my gaze drifted down to my old prison buddy. "Ralph, you have a weird personality, but I really appreciate this."

"I'll get in trouble. Jimmy Joe'll blow a gasket."

"It's a small price to pay. Now, if you'll excuse me, I have to make a lightning dash back to the sale barn. I just hope that Slim hasn't left yet."

"If Jimmy Joe offers to give you a ride, don't take it."

I had to laugh. "Thanks, Ralph. I'll try to remember that. Until we meet again . . ."

I turned myself into the wind, set flaps, lowered the canopy, got clearance from Data Control, pushed the throttle up to Turbo Six, and roared off into the sky. Moments later, I glanced back. Ralph had become a tiny speck, waving good-bye with his paw.

Lucky for me, I didn't encounter enemy aircraft—Buster and Muggs or the dogcatcher—and ten minutes later, I executed a perfect landing in the parking lot of the livestock auction.

Pickups and cattle trucks were leaving when I arrived, so I knew the auction had ended. Was I too late? I ran my gaze over the parking lot. My heart leaped with joy when I saw Slim's pickup, parked exactly where I'd left it . . . when? It seemed days ago, but maybe it had only been a few hours.

I sprinted toward the pickup and dived into the back end, safe and sound in spite of incredible odds. I had survived one of the most harrowing ordeals of my entire career . . . but then I was almost overwhelmed by feelings of great sorrow, for you see, I had failed in my mission to rescue Drover from his own . . . how should I say this? Never mind, I was too sad to be honest.

I glanced around the bed of the pickup and felt its emptiness. My life would never be the same again. It had never been the same before either, but now it would never be the samer.

I felt a rush of tears pressing against my eyeballs and, through the swimming shimmeringness, saw Slim leading his horse out of the sale barn corrals. He loaded the horse into the trailer and came my way. As he passed, he gave me a nod, just as a tear drizzled down my cheek. He climbed into the cab and shut the door.

He hadn't even noticed that our friend, our dear friend, had vanished.

But then, in the aching silence, I heard his voice. "Wait a second." He stepped outside and looked into the hollow emptiness of the lonely pickup bed. "Where's Stub Tail?"

I was fighting back tears but managed to give

him a look that said, "He's missing in action. I'm afraid . . . I'm afraid we've lost him."

Slim scowled and kicked the tire. "Disobedient mutts! That's exactly why I don't bring y'all to town. I tell you to stay in the pickup and . . ." His eyes darted from side to side. He seemed to be thinking. "I wonder . . ." He bent down and looked under the pickup, and a moment later, I heard him say, "Get in the pickup! Good honk, I could have smashed you like a dead skunk in the road!"

Have you figured it out? I couldn't believe it. DROVER HAD SPENT THE WHOLE AFTERNOON, SLEEPING UNDER THE PICKUP!

Well, we needn't go into all the gory details. I was so mad at the little goof-off, I couldn't speak for ten minutes, but by the time we made it back to the ranch, I had screamed myself hoarse. It was kind of an odd situation, to tell you the truth. If I was so glad to get him back, how come I screamed at him for twenty minutes? You figure it out.

Fellers, I threw the book at him. He got twenty-seven Chicken Marks and had to stand with his nose in the corner for three solid hours, and I stood right there to make sure he served every minute of his sentence.

So there you are, the true story of Drover's

Disappearance. He wasn't lost in space or even lost in town. *He was sleeping under the* ...

Oh well. He survived, and in some ways that makes it a happy ending. Life at the ranch returned to normal and ...

This case is closed.

Oh, remember that big parade in town? It really was for me, no kidding.

Have you read all of Hank's adventures?

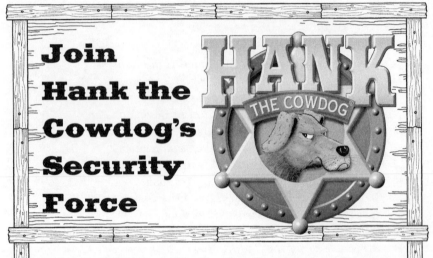

Join Hank the Cowdog's Security Force

Are you a big Hank the Cowdog fan? Then you'll want to join Hank's Security Force. Here is some of the neat stuff you will receive:

Welcome Package
- A Hank paperback of your choice
- A free Hank bookmark

Eight issues of *The Hank Times* with
- Stories about Hank and his friends
- Lots of great games and puzzles
- Special previews of future books
- Fun contests

More Security Force Benefits
- Special discounts on Hank books and audiotapes
- An original Hank poster (19" x 25") absolutely free
- Unlimited access to Hank's Security Force website at www.hankthecowdog.com

Total value of the Welcome Package and *The Hank Times* is $23.95. However, your two-year membership is **only $8.95** plus $4.00 for shipping and handling.

□ Yes, I want to join Hank's Security Force. Enclosed is $12.95 ($8.95 + $4.00 for shipping and handling) for my **two-year membership**. [Make check payable to Maverick Books.]

Which book would you like to receive in your Welcome Package? Choose any book in the series.

(#   )   (#   )
_____
FIRST CHOICE   SECOND CHOICE

                                          BOY or GIRL
_____
YOUR NAME   (CIRCLE ONE)

_____
MAILING ADDRESS

_____
CITY   STATE   ZIP

_____
TELEPHONE   BIRTH DATE

_____
E-MAIL

Are you a □ Teacher or □ Librarian?

Send check or money order for $12.95 to:

Hank's Security Force
Maverick Books
P.O. Box 549
Perryton, Texas 79070

DO NOT SEND CASH. NO CREDIT CARDS ACCEPTED.
Allow 4–6 weeks for delivery.

The Hank the Cowdog Security Force, the Welcome Package, and The Hank Times *are the sole responsibility of Maverick Books. They are not organized, sponsored, or endorsed by Penguin Group (USA) Inc., Puffin Books, Viking Children's Books, or their subsidiaries or affiliates.*